Agnes Mary Frances Robinson

Lyrics - Selected from the Works of A. Mary F. Robinson

Agnes Mary Frances Robinson

Lyrics - Selected from the Works of A. Mary F. Robinson

ISBN/EAN: 9783744787611

Printed in Europe, USA, Canada, Australia, Japan

Cover: Foto ©Andreas Hilbeck / pixelio.de

More available books at **www.hansebooks.com**

Lyrics

Selected from the Works of
A. MARY F. ROBINSON
(Madame James Darmesteter)

CAMEO SERIES

T.FISHER UNWIN   PATERNOSTER SQ.
LONDON E.C. MDCCCXCI

Contents.

[The Lyrics hitherto unpublished are indicated by a star.]

MUSIC :—

CONTENTS.

Music.

B

Music.

BEFORE the dawn is yet the day
  I lie and dream so deep,
So drowsy-deep I cannot say
  If yet I wake or sleep.

But in my dream a tune there is,
  And rings so fresh and sweet
That I would rather die than miss
  The utmost end of it.

And yet I know not an it be
  Some music in the lane,
Or but a song that rose with me
  From sleep, to sink again.

And so, alas, and even so
  I waste my life away;
Nor if the tune be real I know,
  Or but a dream astray.

A Pastoral of Parnassus.

" Ma io perchè venirvi ? O chi 'l concede ? "

AT morning dawn I left my sheep
   And sought the mountains all aglow ;
The shepherds said, " The way is steep :
   Ah, do not go ! "

I left my pastures fresh with rain,
   My water-courses edged with bloom,
A larger breathing space to gain
   And singing room.

Then of a reed I wrought a flute,
   And as I went I sang and played.
But though I sang, my heart was mute
   And sore afraid,

Because the great hill and the sky
   Were full of glooms and glorious
Beyond all light or dark that I
   Imagined thus.

My sense grew pure through love and fear ;
I saw God burn in every briar.
Then sudden voices, strong and clear,
Flashed up like fire.

And turning where that music rang
I saw aloft, half out of sight,
The watching poets ; and they sang
Through day and night.

And very sweet—ah, sweet indeed—
Their voices sounded high and deep.
I blew an echo on my reed
As one asleep.

I heard.   My heart grew cold with dread,
For what would happen if they heard ?
Would not these nightingales strike dead
Their mocking-bird ?

Then from the mountain's steepest crown,
Where white cliffs pierce the tender grass,
I saw an arm reach slowly down,
Heard some word pass.

"The end is come," I thought, "and still
    I am more happy, come what may,
To die upon Parnassus hill
      Than live away."

Then hands and faces luminous
    And holy voices grew one flame—
"Come up, poor singer, and sing with us! '
      They sang; I came.

So ended all my wandering;
    This is the end and this is sweet,—
All night, all day, to listen and sing
      Below their feet.

Going South.

A LITTLE grey swallow,
 I fled to the vales
 Of the nightingales
And the haunts of Apollo.

Behind me lie the sheer white cliffs, the hollow
 Green waves that break at home, the northern
 gales,
 The oaks above the homesteads in the vales,
For all my home is far, and cannot follow.

O nightingale voices !
 O lemons in flower !
 O branches of laurel !

You all are here, but ah not here my choice is :
 Fain would I pluck one pink-vein'd bloom of
 sorrel,
Or watch the wrens build in our hazel bower.

Spring Under Cypresses.

UNDER the cypresses, here in the stony
    Woods of the mountain, the Spring too is
      sunny :
            Rare Spring and early,
            Birds singing sparely,
Pale sea-green hellebore smelling of honey.

Desolate, bright, in the blue Lenten weather,
Cones of the cypresses sparkle together,
            Shining brightly.
            Loosely and lightly,
The winds lift the branches and stir them and
    feather.   .

Where the sun pierces, the sharp boulders glitter
Desolate, bright ; and the white moths flitter
            Pallidly over
            The bells that cover
With faint-smelling green all the fragrant brown
    litter.

Down in the plain the sun ripens for hours—
Look ! in the orchards a mist of pale flowers—
          Past the rose-hedges
          A-bloom to the edges,
A smoke of blue olives, a vision of towers !

Here only hellebore grows, only shade is ;
Surely the very Spring here half afraid is :
          Out of her bosom
          Drops not a blossom,
Mutely she passes through—she and her ladies.

Mutely ?   Ah, no ; for a pause, and thou hearest
One bird who sings alone—one bird, the dearest.
          Nay, who shall name it,
          Call it or claim it ?
Such birds as sing at all sing here their clearest.

Ah, never dream that the brown meadow thrushes,
Finches, or happy larks sing in these hushes.
          Only some poet
          Of birds, flying to it,
Sings here alone, and is lost to the bushes.

La Belle au Bois Dormant.

DOWN the enchanted Forest grey,
   Hark, a dreamy note is borne !
'Tis the winding of a horn
Far away !
   Boughs of oak and boughs of thorn
Stir and sway.

      Yet the wood is haunted,
       Silent many a year ;
      Only long-enchanted
       Dreamers linger here.

'Tis a Forest thick and dim,
   Overgrown and hoar indeed,
   Hung with lichen, choked with weed,
To the brim.
   Sleeps the knight and sleeps the steed
Under him.

      Here the pale princesses
       Lying on the green,
      Pillow with their tresses
       Their enchanted Queen.

Where the barren branches meet
Still they sleep, and none behold
Robes of dim brocaded gold,
Sandalled feet,
Languid arms and lips a-cold
Pale and sweet.

Here the wind is noiseless,
Here the fountain stops,
Hanging blank and voiceless
Her enchanted drops.

Hark, along the unwonted gale
Rings the winding of a horn;
Rings thro' all a world forlorn
Glad Reveil.
Till the blossom studs the thorn,
Thick as hail.

Hark the awaken'd thrushes !
Lo ! the deer awake,
Leaping from the rushes,
Through the windy brake.

Till beneath the flowering tree,
Novel music in her ears,
Lo, asleep a thousand years,

It is She !
　Blow thy clarion, Spring ; she hears !
She is free !

　　　　Break, O bower above her,
　　　　　Briar and thorn divide.
　　　　Hark, the Eternal Lover
　　　　　Calls the Enchanted Bride !

Dawn-Angels.

ALL night I watched awake for morning,
  At last the East grew all a-flame,
The birds for welcome sang, or warning,
  And with their singing morning came.

Along the gold-green heavens drifted
  Pale wandering souls that shun the light,
Whose cloudy pinions torn and rifted,
  Had beat the bars of Heaven all night.

These clustered round the moon, but higher
  A troop of shining spirits went,
Who were not made of wind or fire,
  But some divine dream-element.

Some held the Light, while those remaining
  Shook out their harvest-coloured wings
A faint unusual music raining
  (Whose sound was Light) on earthly things.

They sang, and as a mighty river
  Their voices washed the night away,
From East to West ran one white shiver,
  And waxen strong their song was Day.

A Pastoral.

IT was Whit Sunday yesterday,
　The neighbours met at church to pray;
But I remembered it was May
And went a-wandering far away.

I rested on a shady lawn,
Behind I heard green branches torn,
And through the gap there looked a Faun,
Green ivy hung from either horn.

We built ourselves a flowery house
With roof and walls of tangled boughs,
But while we sat and made carouse
The church bells drowned our songs and vows.

The light died out and left the sky,
We sighed and rose and said good-bye.
We had forgotten—He and I,
That he was dead, that I must die.

Paradise Fancies.

I.

THROUGH Paradise garden
   A minstrel strays,
An old golden viol
   For ever he plays.

Birds fly to his head,
   Beasts lie at his feet,
For none of God's angels
   Make music so sweet.

And here, far from Zion
   And lonely and mute,
I listen and long
   For my heart is the lute.

II.

On the topmost branch of the Tree of Life
   There hung a ripe red apple,
The angels singing underneath
   All praised its crimson dapple.

They plucked it once to play at ball,
  But 'mid the shouts and laughter
The apple fell o'er Heaven's edge,
  Sad angels looking after.

E'en while at ease to see it rest
  Beside a peaceful chapel,
An old priest flung it farther still,
  " Bah, what a battered apple ! "

To a Dragon Fly.

YOU hail from Dream-land, Dragon-fly?
   A stranger hither? so am I,
And (sooth to say) I wonder why
      We either of us came!
Are you (that shine so bright i' the air)
King Oberon's state-messenger?
Come tell me how my old friends fare,
      Is Dream-land still the same?

Who won the latest tourney fight,
King Arthur, or the Red-Cross Knight,
Or he who bore away the bright
      Renown'd Mambrino's Casque?
Is Caliban King's councillor yet?
Cross Mentor jester still and pet?
Is Suckling out of love and debt?
      Has Spenser done his task?

Say, have they settled over there,
Which is the loveliest Guinevere,
Or Gloriana or the fair
      Young Queen of Oberon's Court?

And does Titania torment still
Mike Drayton and sweet-throated Will ?
In sooth of her amours 'twas ill
    To make such merry sport.

Ah, I have been too long away !
No doubt I shall return some day,
But now I'm lost in love and may
    Not leave my Lady's sight.
Mine is (of course) the happier lot,
Yet—tell them I forget them not,
My pretty gay compatriot,
    When you go home to-night.

Celia's Home-Coming.

MAIDENS, kilt your skirts and go
  Down the stormy garden-ways,
Pluck the last sweet pinks that blow,
  Gather roses, gather bays,
Since our Celia comes to-day
That has been too long away.

Crowd her chamber with your sweets—
  Not a flower but grows for her !
Make her bed with linen sheets
  That have lain in lavender ;
Light a fire before she come
Lest she find us chill at home.

Ah, what joy when Celia stands
  By the leaping blaze at last,
Stooping down to warm her hands
  All benumbèd with the blast,
While we hide her cloak away
To assure us she shall stay.

Cyder bring and cowslip wine,
    Fruits and flavours from the East,
Pears and pippins too, and fine
    Saffron loaves to make a feast :
China dishes, silver cups,
For the board where Celia sups !

Then, when all the feasting's done,
    She shall draw us round the blaze,
Laugh, and tell us every one
    Of her far triumphant days—
Celia, out of doors a star,
By the hearth a holier Lar !

Posies.

TO F. M. R.

I.

I MADE a posy for my Love
    As fair as she is soft and fine :
The lilac thrift I made it of,
    And lemon-yellow columbine.

But woe is me for my despair,
    For my pale flowers, woe is me
A bolder man has given her
    A branch of crimson peony !

II.

Come let us a posy make
    Sweet with lasting flowers to-day !
Gather roses, dear, and break
    Pinks in bud and sprigs of bay,
Myrtle, violets, woodruff, rue,
Lavender and featherfew.

Trim it round with southern-wood,
  Grey and sweet as honest age ;
Ladies' bedstraw fresh and good ;
  Lilac thyme and silvery sage.
Kiss it last, and let it lie
With my letters—till it die !

Thanksgiving for Flowers.

YOU bring me flowers—behold my shaded room
  Is grown all glorious and alive with Light.
Moonshine of pallid primroses, and bright
Daffodil-suns that light the way o' the tomb.
You bring me dreams—through sleep's close-lidded
    gloom,
Sad violets mourn for Sappho all the night,
Where purple saffrons make antique delight
Mid crown'd memorials of Narcissus' doom.

A scent of herbs now sets me musing on
Men dead i' the fennel-beds on Marathon :
My flowers, my dreams and I shall lie as dead !
Flowers fade, dreams wake, men die ; but never
    dies
The soul whereby these things were perfected,—
This leaves the world on flower with memories.

Poplar Leaves.

THE wind blows down the dusty street ;
   And through my soul that grieves—
It brings a sudden odour sweet :
   A smell of poplar leaves.

O leaves that herald in the spring,
   O freshness young and pure,
Into my weary soul you bring
   The vigour to endure.

The wood is near, but out of sight,
   Where all the poplars grow ;
Straight up and tall and silver white,
   They quiver in a row.

My love is out of sight, but near ;
   And through my soul that grieves
A sudden memory wafts her here
   As fresh as poplar leaves.

A Rifiorita.

FLOWERS in the wall !
How could he leave the house where
he was born ?
(*We children played together
In warm or wintry weather*)
How could he leave the house where he was
born ?
I count the stones for him and love them all.
(*We children played together
In warm or wintry weather*).

Flowers on the stone !
The Siren loves the sea, but I the Past !
(*We children played together
In warm or wintry weather*)
The Siren loves the sea, but I the Past !
Upon my rock I sing alone, alone,—
(*We children played together
In warm or wintry weather*).

Le Roi Est Mort.

AND shall I weep that Love's no more,
   And magnify his reign?
Sure never mortal man before,
   Would have his grief again.
Farewell the long-continued ache,
   The days a-dream, the nights awake,
I will rejoice and merry make,
   And never more complain.

King Love is dead and gone for aye,
   Who ruled with might and main,
For with a bitter word one day,
   I found my tyrant slain,
And he in Heathenesse was bred,
   Nor ever was baptized, 'tis said,
Nor is of any creed, and dead
   Can never rise again.

Lethe.

COME with me to Lethe-lake,
    Come, since Love is o'er,
He whose thirst those waters slake,
    Thirsteth nevermore.
There the sleepy hemlock grows
    In the night-shade ranks,
Crimson poppies rows on rows
    Flush its quiet banks.

Drink with me of Lethe-lake
    Deep and deeper yet,
Drink with me for dead Love's sake
    Drink till we forget.
Since our roses are all dead,
    Lost our laurel-boughs,
Let these poppies hang instead
    Round our aching brows.

Sonnet.

GOD sent a poet to reform His earth.
  But when he came and found it cold and
    poor,
Harsh and unlovely, where each prosperous boor
Held poets light for all their heavenly birth,
He thought—Myself can make one better worth
The living in than this—full of old lore,
Music and light and love, where Saints adore
And Angels, all within mine own soul's girth.

But when at last he came to die, his soul
Saw earth (flying past to Heaven) with new love,
And all the unused passion in him cried :
O God, your Heaven I know and weary of.
Give me this world to work in and make whole,
God spoke : Therein, fool, thou hast lived and
  died !

Two Lovers.

I.

I LOVE my lover ; on the heights above me
    He mocks my poor attainment with a frown.
I, looking up as he is looking down,
By his displeasure guess he still doth love me ;
For his ambitious love would ever prove me
    More excellent than I as yet am shown :
    So, straining for some good ungrasped, unknown,
I vainly would become his image of me.

And, reaching through the dreadful gulfs that sever
    Our souls, I strive with darkness nights and days,
    Till my perfected work towards him I raise,
Who laughs thereat, and scorns me more than
    ever ;
    Yet his upbraiding is beyond all praise.
This lover that I love I call : Endeavour.

II.

I have another lover loving me,
 Himself beloved of all men, fair and true.
 He would not have me change although I grew
Perfect as Light, because more tenderly
He loves myself than loves what I might be.
 Low at my feet he sings the winter through,
 And, never won, I love to hear him woo.
For in my heaven both sun and moon is he,
 To my bare life a fruitful-flooding Nile,
 His voice like April airs that in our isle
Wake sap in trees that slept since autumn went.
 His words are all caresses, and his smile
The relic of some Eden ravishment;
And he that loves me so I call: Content.

Treasure Song.

THE miser loves to count his store
   Of barren ducats o'er and o'er :
Above all pomp or pleasure
He loves his golden treasure.

And I do love to count alone
A useless treasure of mine own
Heigho ! Delights of dreaming,
So dear, and only seeming !

Love, Death, and Art.

L ORD, give me Love! give me the silent bliss
  Of meeting souls, of answering eyes and hands;
The comfort of one heart that understands;
The thrill and rapture of Love's sealing kiss.
Or grant me—lest I weary of all this—
The quiet of Death's unimagined lands,
Wherein the longed-for Tree of Knowledge stands,
Where Thou art, Lord—and the great mysteries.

Nay let me sing, my God, and I'll forego,
Love's smiling mouth, Death's sweetlier smiling
      eyes.
Better my life long mourn in glorious woe,
Than love unheard in a mute Paradise—
For no grief, no despair, can quail me long,
While I can make these sweet to me in song.

Friendship.

FOR your sovereign sake, my friend,
    All my lovers are estranged,
Shadow lovers without end ;
    But last night they were avenged.

On the middle of the night
    One by one I saw them rise,
Passing in the ghostly light,
    Silent, with averted eyes.

First, my master from the South
    With the laurels round his brow,
And the bitter-smiling mouth,
    Left me—without smiling now.

Then came one long used to rule
    All I was, or did, or had—
Plato, that I read at school
    Till my playmates called me mad.

c *

Maiden saints as pure as pearls,
   Beautiful, divine, austere ;
Sweeter-voiced Æolian girls,
   Left their friend of many a year.

But my earliest friend and best,
   My Beethoven, this was hard,
You should leave me with the rest,
   Pass without one last regard.

For all went and left me there,
   Sighing as they passed me by ;
Ah, how sad their voices were !
   I shall hear them when I die.

" Fare thee well," they said ; "we go
   Scorned as shades and dreams. Adieu !
Love thine earthly friend, but know
   Shadows still thou dost pursue."

Wild Cherry Branches.

I.

LITHE sprays of freshness and faint perfume,
You are strange in a London room ;
Sweet foreigners come to the dull, close city,
Your flowers are memories, clear in the gloom,
That sigh with regret and are fragrant with pity.

II.

Flowers, a week since your long, sweet branches
Swayed, hardly seen, in the dusk overhead ;
(We live, but the bloom on our living is dead).
Ah ! look, where the white moon launches
Her skiff in the skies where the roof-tops spread,

III.

Like rocks on her course. But she rose not so
Through your wavering sprays when the April
    weather
Smelt only of flowers a week ago—
On your stems, in my heart, did such blossoms
    blow !
Let us sigh all together.

IV.

Your sigh is, perchance, for the neighbouring bushes,
With soft, yellow palms, or the song of the thrushes;
But mine for none of the birds that sing,
No flower of the spring,
But for two distant eyes and a voice that hushes.

V.

Such light and music, O blossom,
Was ours when I plucked you one moonrise, and
     you
Remember in fragrance her smile that you knew,
As you lived in her hand, as you lay on her
     bosom
Once, for a moment, and blossomed anew.

VI.

As I took you I looked, half in awe, where my
     friend
Crowned with completeness
All heaven's peace and the whole earth's sweetness;
So does her soul all souls transcend,
So, in my love for her, all loves blend.

VII.

For more than the vast everlasting heaven
Declares in its infinite mute appeal
To hearts that feel,
More than the secret and peace of dim even
Knows of God, may a love reveal.

VIII.

For then indeed it was clear to my soul
That in loving the one I loved the whole,
Fulfilled all aims, attained every goal,
And God was with me, eternity round me,
Though Life still bound me.

IX.

Past is that hour, but the heart's trouble lessens
Because it has been.
When I die, when free of its selfish screen
The god in me soars to the Godhead, the Presence
May seem to it first as the love once seen.

X.

We, flowers, have lived to our blossoming hour,
And not in vain did we rise from the root,
Whether we perish or ripen to power;
We know what sweetness it is to flower,
Let life or death be the fruit.

The Springs of Fontana.

THE springs of Fontana well high on the moun-
    tain,
Out of the rock of the granite they pour
       Twenty or more ;
Ripple and runnel and freshet and fountain
Well, happy tears, from the heart of the mountain
       Up at Fontana.

See, not a step can we take but a spring
Breaks from the roots of the blond-flower'd chest-
    nuts—
(Look, in the water their long golden breast-knots
Flung in caress !)—from a tuft of the ling,
       From a stone, anything,
       Up at Fontana.

Twenty or more, and no one of the twenty
Gushes the same ; here the waters abundant
       Babble redundant,
Filling the vale with the bruit of their plenty ;
Here a mere ripple, a trickle, a scanty
       Dew on Fontana.

Surely one noonday the Prophet in heaven
Slept, and the wand of the desert fell—
Fell to the rock, and the rock was riven.
Lo, all around it eternally well
      (A miracle!)
    The springs of Fontana.

    Waters of boon!
Deluge or drought cannot alter your current,
Swift in December and icy in June,
Full when the icicle hangs on the torrent,
Full when the river is dry and the noon
    Parches Fontana.

    Over the rocks!
Over the tree-root that tangles and blocks—
Robbing from all that resists you a sunny
Scent of the cistus and rock-hidden honey,
Yarrow, campanula, thyme, agrimony—
    Flow from Fontana!

Flow, happy waters, and gather and rally,
    Rush to the plain.
Flow to the heavenly fields of Limain,
Blue as a dream in the folds of the valley;
Feed them and fatten with blossom and grain,
    Springs of Fontana!

River of springs,
Born many times in renewal unending,
Bright, irresistible, purest of things,
Blessing the rocks that oppose you, befriending
Pastures and cattle and men in your wending
Forth from Fontana.

Born (who knows how?) a mysterious fountain
Out of the stone and the dust of the mountain,
Bound to a country we know little of,
How shall I bless ye and praise ye enough,
Image of Love,
Springs of Fontana!

July, 1889.

" Un coeur tendre qui hait le néant vaste et noir
Du passé lumineux recueille tout vestige."

Rosa Rosarum.

Rosa Rosarum.

G IVE me, O friend, the secret of thy heart
Safe in my breast to hide,
So that the leagues which keep our lives apart
May not our souls divide.

Give me the secret of thy life to lay
Asleep within my own,
Nor dream that it shall mock thee any day
By any sign or tone.

Nay, as in walking through some convent-close,
Passing beside a well,
Oft have we thrown a red and scented rose
To watch it as it fell ;

Knowing that never more the rose shall rise
To shame us, being dead ;
Watching it spin and dwindle till it lies
At rest, a speck of red—

'Thus, I beseech thee, down the silent deep
   And darkness of my heart,
Cast thou a rose; give me a rose to keep,
   My friend, before we part.

For, as thou passest down thy garden-ways,
   Many a blossom there
Groweth for thee : lilies and laden bays,
   And rose and lavender.

But down the darkling well one only rose
   In all the year is shed ;
And o'er that chill and secret wave it throws
   A sudden dawn of red.

Florentine May.

STILL, still is the Night; still as the pause after
pain ;
   Still and as dear ;
Deep, solemn, immense ; veiling the stars in the
clear
Thrilling and luminous blue of the moon-shot
atmosphere ;
   Ah, could the Night remain !

Who, truly, shall say thou art sullen or dark or
unseen,
   Thou, O heavenly Night,
Clear o'er the valley of olives asleep in the quivering
light,
Clear o'er the pale-red hedge of the rose, and the
lilies all white
   Down at my feet in the green ?

Nay, not as the Day, thou art light, O Night, with
a beam
   Far more dear and divine ;

Never the noon was blue as these tremulous heavens
  of thine,
Pulsing with stars half seen, and vague in a pallid
  shine,
    Vague as a dream.

Night, clear with the moon, filled with the dreamy
  fire
    Shining in thicket and close,
Fire from the lamp in his breast that the luminous
  fire-fly throws;
Night, full of wandering light and of song, and the
  blossoming rose,
    Night, be thou my desire!

Night, Angel of Night, hold me and cover me so—
    Open thy wings!
Ah, bend above and embrace!—till I hear in the
  one bird that sings
The throb of thy musical heart in the dusk, and the
  magical things
    Only the Night can know.

Serenade.

M OON of my soul, arise !
  Ah me, the moon, the moon goes out in
    clouds ;
  Lo, a great darkness all the heaven
    shrouds
And night is in mine eyes.

Star of my life, appear !
  Ah, not a star, not one is lit on high—
  Only along the edges of the sky
There slants a falling sphere.

Invocations.

O SONG in the nightingale's throat, O music,
    Dropt as it fell by a falling star,—
All of the silence is filled with thy pain,
Listening till it shall echo again.
    O song in the nightingale's throat, O music,
      Thou art the soul of the silence afar !

O space of the moon in the starless heaven,
    Raining a whiteness on moorland and sea,
Falling as lightly and purely as dew,
All of the shadow thou filterest through—
    O space of the moon in the starless heaven,
      Surely the night is the shadow of thee !

O silence of Death, O world of darkness,
    When over me the last shadow shall fall,
Holdest thou safe in the night all around
Any moon to arise, any music to sound ?
    O silence of Death, O world of darkness,
      Shall we perceive thee or know thee at all ?

Aubade Triste.

THE last pale rank of poplar-trees
   Begins to glimmer into light,
With stems and branches faintly white
Against a heaven one dimly sees
   Beyond the failing night.

A point of grey that grows to green
   Fleck'd o'er with rainy yellow bars,—
A sudden whitening of the stars,
A pallor where the moon has been,
   A peace the morning mars ;

When, lo ! a shiver of the breeze
   And all the ruffled birds awake,
The rustling aspens stir and shake ;
For, pale, beyond the pallid trees,
   The dawn begins to break.

And now the air turns cool and wan,
   A drizzling rain begins to fall,
The sky clouds over with a pall—
The night, that was for me, is gone ;
   The day has come for all.

A Jonquil.

IN THE PISAN CAMPO SANTO.

OUT of the place of death,
　　Out of the cypress shadow,
Out of sepulchral earth,
　　Dust that Calvary gave;
Sprang, as fragrant of breath
　　As any flower of the meadow,
This, with death in its birth,
　　Sent like speech from the grave.

So, in a world of doubt,
　　Love—like a flower—
Blossoms suddenly white,
　　Suddenly sweet and pure;
Shedding a breath about
　　Of new mysterious power;
Lifting a hope in the night,
　　Not to be told, but sure.

A Song.

L AST night I met mine own true love
    Walking in Paradise,
A halo shone above his hair,
    A glory in his eyes.

We sat and sang in alleys green
    And heard the angels play ;
Believe me, this was true last night
    Though it is false to-day.

Stornelli and Strambotti.

I.

FLOWER of the vine !
    I scarcely knew or saw how love
    began ;
So mean a flower brings forth the sweetest wine !

*   *   *   *   *

O mandolines that thrill the moonlit street,
    O lemon flowers so faint and freshly blown,
O seas that lap a solemn music sweet
    Through all the pallid night against the stone,
O lovers tramping past with happy feet,
    O heart that hast a memory of thine own—
For Mercy's sake no more, no more repeat
    The word it is so hard to hear alone !

*   *   *   *   *

Flowers in the hay !
My heart and all the fields are full of flowers ;
So tall they grow before the mowing-day.

II.

Rose in the rain !
We part ; I dare not look upon your tears :
So frail, so white, they shatter and they stain.

* * * * *

Love is a bird that breaks its voice with singing,
 Love is a rose blown open till it fall,
Love is a bee that dies of its own stinging,
 And Love the tinsel cross upon a pall.
Love is the Siren, towards a quicksand bringing
 Enchanted fishermen that hear her call.
Love is a broken heart,—Farewell,—the wringing
 Of dying hands. Ah, do not love at all !

* * * * *

Tuscan Olives.

(SEVEN RISPETTI.)

I.

THE colour of the olives who shall say ?
  In winter on the yellow earth they're blue,
A wind can change the green to white or gray,
  But they are olives still in every hue ;

But they are olives always, green or white,
As love is love in torment or delight ;
But they are olives, ruffled or at rest,
As love is always love in tears or jest.

II.

We walked along the terraced olive-yard,
  And talked together till we lost the way ;
We met a peasant, bent with age and hard,
  Bruising the grape-skins in a vase of clay ;

Bruising the grape-skins for the second wine.
We did not drink, and left him, Love of mine ;
Bruising the grapes already bruised enough :
He had his meagre wine, and we our love.

III.

We climbed one morning to the sunny height
  Where chestnuts grow no more and olives
    grow ;
Far-off the circling mountains cinder-white,
  The yellow river and the gorge below.

" Turn round," you said, O flower of Paradise ;
I did not turn, I looked upon your eyes.
" Turn round," you said, "turn round, look at the
    view ! "
I did not turn, my Love, I looked at you.

IV.

How hot it was ! Across the white-hot wall
  Pale olives stretch towards the blazing street ;
You broke a branch, you never spoke at all,
  But gave it me to fan with in the heat ;

You gave it me without a sign or word,
And yet, my love, I think you knew I heard.
You gave it me without a word or sign :
Under the olives first I called you mine.

V.

At Lucca, for the autumn festival,
　The streets are tulip-gay ; but you and I
Forgot them, seeing over church and wall
　Guinigi's tower soar i' the black-blue sky ;

A stem of delicate rose against the blue ;
And on the top two lonely olives grew,
Crowning the tower, far from the hills, alone ;
As on our risen love our lives are grown.

VI.

Who would have thought we should stand again
　　together,
　Here, with the convent a frown of towers above
　　us ;
Here, mid the sere-wooded hills and wintry
　　weather ;
　Here, where the olives bend down and seem to
　　love us ;

Here, where the fruit-laden olives half remember
All that began in their shadow last November ;
Here, where we knew we must part, must part and
　　sever ;
Here, where we know we shall love for aye and
　　ever.

VII.

Reach up and pluck a branch, and give it me,
  That I may hang it in my Northern room,
That I may find it there, and wake and see
  —Not you ! not you !—dead leaves and wintry
    gloom.

O senseless olives, wherefore should I take
Your leaves to balm a heart that can but ache ?
Why should I take you hence, that can but show
How much is left behind?   I do not know.

D *

Apprehension

I.

O FOOLISH dream, to hope that such as I
    Who answer only to thine easiest moods,
  Should fill thy heart, as o'er my heart there
    broods
The perfect fulness of thy memory !
I flit across thy soul as white birds fly
. Across the untrodden desert solitudes :
    A moment's flash of wings ; fair interludes
That leave unchanged the eternal sand and sky.

Even such to thee am I ; but thou to me
As the embracing shore to the sobbing sea,
    Even as the sea itself to the stone-tossed rill.
But who, but who shall give such rest to thee ?
The deep mid-ocean waters perpetually
    Call to the land, and call unanswered still.

II.

As dreams the fasting nun of Paradise,
  And finds her gnawing hunger pass away
  In thinking of the happy bridal day
That soon shall dawn upon her watching eyes ;
So, dreaming of your love, do I despise
  Harshness or death of friends, doubt, slow decay,
  Madness,—all dreads that fill me with dismay
And creep about me oft with fell surmise.

For you are true, and all I hoped you are,
  O perfect answer to my calling heart !
  And very sweet my life is, having thee.
Yet must I dread the dim end shrouded far ;
  Yet must I dream : should once the good planks
    start,
  How bottomless yawns beneath the boiling sea !

Adam and Eve.

WHEN Adam fell asleep in Paradise
  He made himself a helpmeet as he
   dreamed ;
And, lo ! she stood before his waking eyes,
 And was the woman that his vision seemed.

She knelt beside him there in tender awe
  To find the living fountain of her soul,
And so in either's eyes the other saw
  The light they missed in Heaven, and knew the
   goal.

Thrice-blessed Adam, husband of thine Eve !
  She brought thee for her dowry death and
   shame ;
She taught thee one may worship and deceive ;
  But yet thy dream and she were still the same ;
Nor ever in the desert turned thine eyes
Towards Lilith by the brooks of Paradise.

Love Without Wings.

EIGHT SONGS.

I.

I THOUGHT : no more the worst endures !
   I die, I end the strife,—
You swiftly took my hands in yours
And drew me back to life !

II

We sat when shadows darken,
   And let the shadows be :
Each was a soul to hearken,
   Devoid of eyes to see.

You came at dusk to find me ;
   I knew you well enough . . .
O Lights that dazzle and blind me—
   It is no friend, but Love !

III.

How is it possible
　　You should forget me,
Leave me for ever
　　And never regret me !

I was the soul of you,
　　Past Love or Loathing,
Lost in the whole of you . . .
　　Now, am I nothing ?

IV.

The fallen oak still keeps its yellow leaves
　　But all its growth is o'er !
So, at your name, my heart still beats and grieves,
　　Although I love no more.

V.

And so I shall meet you
　　Again, my dear ;
How shall I greet you ?
　　What shall I hear ?

I, you forgot !
　　(But who shall say
You loved me not
　　—Yesterday ?)

VI.

Ah me, do you remember still
  The garden where we strolled together,
The empty groves, the little hill
  Starred o'er with pale Italian heather ?

And you to me said never a word,
  Nor I a single word to you.
And yet how sweet a thing was heard,
  Resolved, abandoned, by us two !

VII.

I know you love me not . . . I do not love you ;
  Only at dead of night
I smile a little, softly dreaming of you
  Until the dawn is bright.

I love you not ; you love me not ; I know it !
  But when the day is long
I haunt you like the magic of a poet,
  And charm you like a song.

VIII.

O Death of things that are, Eternity
  Of things that seem !
Of all the happy past remains to me,
  To-day, a dream !

Long blessèd days of love and wakening thought,
  All, all are dead ;
Nothing endures we did, nothing we wrought,
  Nothing we said.

But once I dreamed I sat and sang with you
  On Ida hill.
There, in the echoes of my life, we two
  Are singing still.

Tuscan Cypress.

(SIXTEEN RISPETTI.)

I.

MY mother bore me 'neath the streaming moon,
And all the enchanted light is in my soul.
I have no place amid the happy noon,
I have no shadow there nor aureole.

Ah, lonely whiteness in a clouded sky,
You are alone, nor less alone am I ;
Ah, moon, that makest all the roses grey,
The roses I behold are wan as they !

II.

What good is there, Ah me, what good in Love ?
Since, even if you love me, we must part ;
And since for either, and you cared enough,
There's but division and a broken heart ?

And yet, God knows, to hear you say : My Dear !
I would lie down and stretch me on the bier.
And yet would I, to hear you say : My own !
With mine own hands drag down the burial stone.

III.

I love you more than any words can say,
  And yet you do not feel I love you so ;
And slowly I am dying day by day,—
  You look at me, and yet you do not know.

You look at me, and yet you do not fear :
You do not see the mourners with the bier.
You answer when I speak and wish me well,
And still you do not hear the passing bell.

IV.

O Love, O Love, come over the sea, come here,
  Come back and kiss me once when I am dead !
Come back and lay a rose upon my bier,
  Come, light the tapers at my feet and head.

Come back and kiss me once upon the eyes,
So I, being dead, shall dream of Paradise;
Come, kneel beside me once and say a prayer,
So shall my soul be happy anywhere.

V.

I sowed the field of Love with many seeds,
  With many sails I sailed before the blast,
And all my crop is only bitter weeds ;
  My sails are torn, the winds have split the mast.

All of the winds have torn my sails and shattered,
All of the winds have blown my seed and scat-
tered,
All of the storms have burst on my endeavour,—
So let me sleep at last and sleep for ever.

VI.

I am so pale to-night, so mere a ghost,
  Ah, what, to-morrow, shall my spirit be ?
No living angel of the heavenly host,
  No happy soul, blithe in eternity.

Oh, I shall wander on beneath the moon
A lonely phantom seeking for you, soon ;
A wandering ghost, seeking you timidly,
Whom you will tremble, dear, and start to see !

VII.

When I am dead and I am quite forgot,
  What care I if my spirit lives or dies ?
To walk with angels in a grassy plot,
  And pluck the lilies grown in Paradise ?

Ah, no ! the heaven of all my heart has been
To hear your voice and catch the sighs between.
Ah, no ! the better heaven I fain would give,
But in a cranny of your soul to live.

VIII.

Ah me, you well might wait a little while,
　And not forget me, Sweet, until I die !
I had a home, a little distant isle,
　With shadowy trees and tender misty sky.

I had a home !　It was less dear than thou,
And I forgot, as you forget me now.
I had a home, more dear than I could tell,
And I forgot, but now remember well.

IX.

Love me to-day and think not on to-morrow !
　Come, take my hands, and lead me out of doors,
There in the fields let us forget our sorrow,
　Talking of Venice and Ionian shores ;—

Talking of all the seas innumerable
Where we will sail and sing when I am well ;
Talking of Indian roses gold and red,
Which we will plait in wreaths—when I am dead.

X.

There is a Siren in the middle sea
　Sings all day long and wreathes her pallid hair.
Seven years you sail, and seven ceaselessly,
　From any port ere you adventure there.

Thither we'll go, and thither sail away
Out of the world, to hear the Siren play !
Thither we'll go and hide among her tresses,
Since all the world is savage wildernesses.

XI.

Tell me a story, dear, that is not true,
   Strange as a vision, full of splendid things ;
Here will I lie and dream it is not you,
   And dream it is a mocking bird that sings.

For if I find your voice in any part,
Even the sound of it will break my heart ;
For if you speak of us and of our love,
I faint and die to feel the thrill thereof.

XII.

Let us forget we loved each other much,
   Let us forget we ever have to part,
Let us forget that any look or touch
   Once let in either to the other's heart.

Only we'll sit upon the daisied grass
And hear the larks and see the swallows pass ;
Only we'll live awhile, as children play,
Without to-morrow, without yesterday.

XIII.

Far, far away and in the middle sea—
  So still I dream, although the dream is vain,—
There lies a valley full of rest for me,
  Where I shall live and you shall love again.

O ships that sail, O masts against the sky,
Will you not stop awhile in passing by?
O prayers that hope, O faith that never knew,
Will you not take me on to heaven with you?

XIV.

Flower of the Cypress, little bitter bloom,
  You are the only blossom left to gather ;
I never prized you, grown amid the gloom,
  But well you last, though all the others wither.

Flower of the Cypress, I will bind a crown
Tight round my brows to still these fancies down.
Flower of the Cypress, I will tie a wreath
Tight round my breast to kill the heart beneath.

XV.

Ah, Love, I cannot die, I cannot go
  Down in the dark and leave you all alone !
Ah, hold me fast, safe in the warmth I know,
  And never shut me underneath a stone.

Dead in the grave !   And I can never hear
If you are ill or if you miss me, Dear.
Dead, oh my God ! and you may need me yet,
While I shall sleep ; while I—while *I*—forget !

XVI.

Come away Sorrow, Sorrow come away—
   Let us go sit in some cool, shadowy place ;
There shall you sing and hush me all the day,
   While I will dream about my lover's face.

Hush me, O Sorrow, like a babe to sleep,
Then close the lids above mine eyes that weep ;
Rock me, O Sorrow, like a babe in pain,
Nor, when I slumber, wake me up again.

Arnold Von Winkelried.

THE great things that I love I cannot do,
  The little things I do I cannot love !
Far from the goal I wander, and above
The voice is mute of Him I never knew.

Nothing is sweet, I find, and nothing true,
  And none of all my dreams is dear enough—
  And only one is worth the dreaming of ;
If I could give my life and die for you !

O easy death, surrounded with alarms,
  Blue ranks of serried spears that swerve and
      start
    Where heroes clench their eyes and catch their
      breath !
To clasp a score of lances in my arms
  And turn them from your front deep in my
      heart
    And die, and do you service in my death !

Night.

O NIGHT eternal and blue,
  Holy and soft above,
You seem to lay on my forehead
  The touch of an infinite love—

The touch of a love that never
  Will understand me aright—
Why should you touch me and love me,
  O tender and delicate night ?

O night, look in with your stars
  On the wintry face of despair,
And your stars will eddy and shrivel
  As leaves in a gust of the air !

E

Honour.

ONE star at least, one star still breaks the
    night,
Sinister, pallid, as the peace of death ;
And through the rain and wind a little light
    Streams fitfully across the windy heath.

All round me from the towering seas beneath
    Atlantic billows dash their storms of white;
Among the rocks the angry waters seethe ;—
    In heaven my star, my star is out of sight !

Yet shine again O white Divinity,
    And wheresoe'er thou leadest I will go—
What, down ?   Over the cliff's edge ?
                  Forth and down ?

There shines the path I follow ! yet I know
    The infamous blind creatures of the sea
    Swim dimly with wide faces where I drown.

Semitones.

I.

GIVE me a rose not merely sweet and fresh,
    Not only red and bright,
But caught about in such a thorny mesh
    As rankles in delight.

Smile on me, Sweet ; but look not only kind :
    The smile that most endears
Trembles on pallid lips from eyes half-blind
    With brine of bitter tears.

II.

    Ah, could I clasp thee in mine arms,
        And thou not feel me there,
    Asleep and free from vain alarms,
        Asleep and unaware !

    Ah, could I kiss thy pallid cheek,
        And thou not know me nigh ;
    Asleep at last, and very meek,
        Who wert as proud as I.

III.

We did not dream, my Heart, and yet
  With what a pang we woke at last !
  We were not happy in the past
It is so bitter to forget.

We did not hope, my Soul, for Heaven ;
  Yet now the hour of death is nigh,
  How hard, how strange it is to die
Like leaves along the tempest driven.

An Oasis.

YOU wandered in the desert waste, athirst ;
My soul I gave you as a well to drink ;
A little while you lingered at the brink,
And then you went, nor either blessed nor cursed.

The image of your face, which sank that day
Into the magic waters of the well,
Still haunts their clearness, still remains to tell
Of one who looked and drank and could not stay.

The sun shines down, the moon slants over it,
The stars look in and are reflected not ;
Only your face, unchanged and unforgot,
Shines through the deeps, till all the waves are lit.

My soul I gave you as a well to drink,
And in its depth your face is clearer far
Than any shine of sun or moon or star—
Since then you pause by many a greener brink.

Tuberoses.

I.

THE Tuberose you left me yesterday
    Leans yellowing in the glass we set it in ;
It could not live when you were gone away,
    Poor spike of withering sweetness changed and
        thin.

And all the fragrance of the dying flower
    Is grown too faint and poisoned at the source,
Like passion that survives a guilty hour,
    To find its sweetness heavy with remorse.

What shall we do, my dear, with dying roses ?
    Shut them in weighty tomes where none will
        look
—To wonder when the unfrequent page uncloses
    Who shut the wither'd blossoms in the book ?—

What shall we do, my dear, with things that perish,
    Memory, roses, love we feel and cherish ?

II.

Alive and white, we praised the Tuberose,
  So sweet it fill'd the garden with its breath,
A spike of waxy bloom that grows and grows
  Until at length it blooms itself to death.

Everything dies that lives—everything dies;
  How shall we keep the flower we lov'd so long?
O press to death the transient thing we prize,
  Crush it, and shut the elixir in a song.

A song is neither live nor sweet nor white;
  It hath no heavenly blossom tall and pure,
No fragrance can it breathe for our delight,
  It grows not, neither lives; it may endure.

Sweet Tuberose, adieu! you fade too fast!
  Only a dream, only a thought, can last.

III.

Who'd stay to muse if Death could never wither?
  Who dream a dream if Passion did not pass?
But, once deceived, poor mortals, hasten hither
  To watch the world in Fancy's magic glass.

Truly your city, O men, hath no abiding !
   Built on the sand it crumbles, as it must ;
And as you build, above your praise and chiding,
   The columns fall to crush you to the dust.

But fashion'd in the mirage of a dream,
   Having nor life nor sense, a bubble of nought,
The enchanted City of the Things that Seem
   Keeps till the end of time the eternal Thought.

Forswear to-day, forswearing joy and sorrow,
Forswear to-day, O man, and take to-morrow.

In Affliction.

I WATCH the happier people of the house
  Come in and out, and talk, and go their
    ways ;
I sit and gaze at them ; I cannot rouse
  My heavy mind to share their busy days.

I watch them glide, like skaters on a stream,
  Across the brilliant surface of the world.
But I am underneath : they do not dream
  How deep below the eddying flood is whirl'd.

They cannot come to me, nor I to them ;
  But, if a mightier arm could reach and save,
Should I forget the tide I had to stem ?
  Should I, like these, ignore the abysmal wave ?

Yes ! in the radiant air how could I know
How black it is, how fast it is, below.

Remembrance.

O NIGHT of Death, O night that bringest all !
  Night full of dreams and large with promises,
  O night that holdest on thy shadowy knees
Sleep for all fevers, hope for every thrall ;

Bring thou to my belovèd, when I die,
  The memory of our enchanted past ;
  So let her turn, remembering me at last,
And I shall hear and triumph where I lie.

Then let my face, pale as a waning moon,
  Rise on thy dark and be again as dear ;
Let my dead voice find its forgotten tune
  And strike again as sweetly on her ear
As when, upon my lips, one far-off June,
  Thy name, O Death ! she could not brook to
    hear.

Art and Life.

(A SONNET.)

WHEN autumn comes, my orchard trees alone
    Shall bear no fruit to deck the reddening
      year—
When apple gatherers climb the branches sere
Only on mine no harvest shall be grown.
For when the pearly blossom first was blown,
    I filled my hands with delicate buds and dear,
    I dipped them in thine icy waters clear,
O well of Art! and turned them all to stone.

Therefore, when winter comes, I shall not eat
Of mellow apples such as others prize :
    I shall go hungry in a magic spring !—
All round my head and bright before mine eyes
The barren, strange, eternal blossoms meet,
    While I, not less an-hungered, gaze and sing.

Temple Garlands.

THERE is a temple in my heart
    Where moth or rust can never come,
A temple swept and set apart
    To make my soul a home;

And round about the doors of it
    Hang garlands that for ever last,
That gathered once are always sweet;
    The roses of the Past !

Pallor.

THE great white lilies in the grass
    Are pallid as the smile of death ;
For they remember still—alas !—
    The graves they sprang from underneath.

The angels up in heaven are pale—
    For all have died, when all is said ;
Nor shall the lutes of Eden avail
    To let them dream they are not dead.

Song.

I HAVE lost my singing-voice ;
  My heyday's over.
No more I lilt my cares and joys,
  But keep them under cover.
  My heyday's gone :
  I sit and look on.
Life rushes past with a sob and a moan.

Wherefore should I care to tell
  The pang that rends me ?
If it leave me all is well ;
  And if it last it ends me.
  The tears that rise
  To my entrancèd eyes
Drop for a world full of hunger and sighs.

Personality.

(A SESTINA.)

A S one who goes between high garden walls,
  Along a road that never has an end,
With still the empty way behind, in front,
Which he must pace for evermore alone—
So, even so, is Life to every soul,
Walled in with barriers that no Love can break.

And yet, ah me! how often would we break
Through every fence, and overleap the walls,
And link ourselves to some belovèd soul,
Hearing her answering voice until the end,
Going her chosen way, no more alone,
But happy comrades, seeing Heaven in front.

But, ah, the barrier's high! and still my front
I dash against the stones in vain, nor break
A passage through, but still remain alone :
Hearing sometimes across the garden walls
A voice the wind brings over, or an end
Of song that sinks like dew into my soul.

Since others sing, let me forget, my Soul,
How dreary-long the road goes on in front,
And tow'rds how flat, inevitable an end.
Come, let me look for daisies, let me break
The gillyflowers that shelter in the walls—
But, ah ! it is so sad to be alone !

For ever, irremediably alone,
Not only I or thou, but every soul,
Each cased and fastened with invisible walls.
Shall we go mad with it ? or bear a front
Of desperate courage doomed to fail and break ?
Or trudge in sullen patience till the end ?

Ah, hope of every heart, there *is* an end !
An end when each shall be no more alone,
But either dead, or strong enough to break
This prisoning self and find that larger Soul
(Neither of thee nor me) enthroned in front
Of Time, beyond the world's remotest walls !

I trust the end and sing within my walls,
Sing all alone, to bid some listening soul
Wait till the day break, watch for me in front !

Stars.

The Stars.

(To J. D.)

SESTINA.

STARS in the sky, fold upon fold of stars !
    And still beyond the stars those gulfs of air
Flecked soft and pale with milkier stars beyond,
Millions of miles above our dusky world :
Pale stars, whose light down the unplumbed abyss
Falls, ere it reach us, through a thousand years.

There was a God in the unwritten years
Who lit the flaming order of the stars :
Let there be Light ! He said, and lo ! the abyss
Grew live and tremulous with rustling air,
Grew bright with stars and moons, and each a
    world
Shining, a light to other worlds beyond.

O were you even as we, bright orbs beyond
Who shine and shed your glory all these years,
Not light, but smoke would fall from every world ;
Smoke, black with human evil, black, O stars
With His neglect who lit the sparkling air ;
But left within—unformed and void—the Abyss.

O stars that dance indifferent in the Abyss,
Our Earth may seem as bright to you beyond ;
Yourselves, to them that breathe your delicate air,
As desolate ; Life in the Lunar years
As long ; and the straight rivers of the stars
And primal snows divide as drear a world.

And men, perchance, as we, in every world
Fill with their dreams the bright and vast abyss :
A Christ has died in vain on all the stars,
And each, unhappy, seeks a star beyond
Where God rewards the dead through endless
    years. . . .
And so we circle, dumb, in the silent air.

What shall we find more holy in all the air ?
Lo, when the first huge, incandescent world
Burst out of Chaos and flamed a million years,
Until, with too much flaming, thro' the abyss
Flake after flake dropped off and flamed be-
    yond :—
That was the God who lit the host of stars !

For Light, the stars ; for breath, the realms of air ;
For Hope, beyond this dark and suffering world,
Nought in the Abyss, nor ought in the endless
    years.

Etruscan Tombs.

I

TO think the face we love shall ever die,
 And be the indifferent earth, and know us
  not !
To think that one of us shall live to cry
 On one long buried in a distant spot !

O wise Etruscans, faded in the night
 Yourselves, with scarce a rose-leaf on your trace ;
You kept the ashes of the dead in sight,
 And shaped the vase to seem the vanished face.

But, O my Love, my life is such an urn
 That tender memories mould with constant
  touch,
Until the dust and earth of it they turn
 To your dear image that I love so much :

A sacred urn, filled with the sacred past,
That shall recall you while the clay shall last.

II.

These cinerary urns with human head
   And human arms that dangle at their sides,
The earliest potters made them for their dead,
   To keep the mother's ashes or the bride's.

O rude attempt of some long-spent despair—
   With symbol and with emblem discontent—
To keep the dead alive and as they were,
   The actual features and the glance that went!

The anguish of your art was not in vain,
   For lo, upon these alien shelves removed
The sad immortal images remain,
   And show that once they lived and once you
      loved.

But oh, when I am dead may none for me
Invoke so drear an immortality!

III.

Beneath the branches of the olive yard
   Are roots where cyclamen and violet grow
Beneath the roots the earth is deep and hard
   And there a king was buried long ago.

The peasants digging deeply in the mould
  Cast up the autumn soil about the place,
And saw a gleam of unexpected gold,
  And underneath the earth a living face.

With sleeping lids and rosy lips he lay
  Among the wreaths and gems that mark the
    king
One moment; then a little dust and clay
  Fell shrivelled over wreath and urn and ring.

A carven slab recalls his name and deeds,
Writ in a language no man living reads.

IV.

Here lies the tablet graven in the past,
  Clear-charactered and firm and fresh of line.
See, not a word is gone; and yet how fast
  The secret no man living may divine!

What did he choose for witness in the grave?
  A record of his glory on the earth?
The wail of friends? The Pæans of the brave?
  The sacred promise of the second birth?

The tombs of ancient Greeks in Sicily
  Are sown with slender discs of graven gold

Filled with the praise of Death : " Thrice happy
   he
  Wrapt in the milk-soft sleep of dreams untold!"

They sleep their patient sleep in altered lands,
The golden promise in their fleshless hands.

Venetian Nocturne.

DOWN the narrow Calle where the moonlight
cannot enter,
  The houses are so high ;
Silent and alone we pierced the night's dim core
and centre—
  Only you and I.

Clear and sad our footsteps rang along the hollow
pavement,
  Sounding like a bell ;
Sounding like a voice that cries to souls in Life's
enslavement,
  " There is Death as well ! "

Down the narrow dark we went, until a sudden
whiteness
  Made us hold our breath ;
All the white Salute towers and domes in moonlit
brightness,—
  Ah ! could this be Death ?

The Dead Friend.

I.

WHEN you were alive, at least,
  There were days I never met you.
In the study, at the feast,
  By the hearth, I could forget you.

Moods there were of many days
  When, methinks, I did not mind you.
Now, oh now, in any place
  Wheresoe'er I go, I find you!

You . . . but how profoundly changed,
  O you dear-belov'd dead woman!
Made mysterious and estranged,
  All-pervading, superhuman.

Ah! to meet you as of yore,
  Kind, alert, and quick to laughter:
You, the friend I loved Before;
  Not this tragic friend of After.

II.

The house was empty where you came no more;
  I sat in awe and dread;
When, lo! I heard a hand that shook the door,
  And knew it was the Dead.

One moment—ah !—the anguish took my side,
  The fainting of the will.
" God of the living, leave me not ! " I cried,
  And all my flesh grew chill.

One moment; then I opened wide my heart
  And open flung the door :
"What matter whence thou comest, what thou
    art ?—
Come to me ! " . . . Never more

III.

They lie at peace, the darkness fills
  The hollow of their empty gaze.,
The dust falls in their ears and stills
  The echo of our fruitless days ;

The earth takes back their baser part ;
  The brain no longer bounds the dream ;
The broken vial of the heart
  Lets out its passion in a stream.

And in this silence that they have
  One inner vision grows more bright ;
The Dead remember in the grave
  As I remember here to-night.

(1890.)

Sonnet.

SINCE childhood have I dragged my life along
    The dusty purlieus and approach of Death,
    Hoping the years would bring me easier breath,
And turn my painful sighing to a song ;
But, ah, the years have done me cruel wrong,
    For they have robbed me of that happy faith ;
    Still in the world of men I move a wraith,
Who to the shadow-world not yet belong.

Too long, indeed, I linger here and take
    The room of others but to droop and sigh ;
Wherefore, O spinning sisters, for my sake,
    No more the little tangled knots untie ;
But all the skein, I do beseech you, break,
    And spin a stronger thread more perfectly.

Song.

OH for the wings of a dove,
  To fly far away from my own soul,
  Reach and be merged in the vast whole
Heaven of infinite Love!

Oh that I were as the rain,
  To fall and be lost in the great sea,
  One with the waves, till the drowned Me
Might not be severed again!

Infinite arms of the air,
  Surrounding the stars and without strife
  Blending our life with their large life,
Lift me and carry me there!

A Classic Landscape.

THIS wood might be some Grecian heritage
   Of the antique world, this hoary ilex wood ;
So broad the shade, so deep the solitude,
So grey the air where Oread fancies brood.

Beyond, the fields are tall with purple sage ;
   The sky bends downward like a purple sheet—
A purple wind-filled sail—i' the noonday heat ;
And past the river shine the fields of wheat.

O tender wheat, O starry saxifrage,
   O deep-red tulips, how the fields are fair !
Far off the mountains pierce the quivering air,
Ash-coloured, mystical, remote, and bare.

How far they look, the Mountains of Mirage
   Or northern Hills of Heaven, how far away !
In front the long paulonia-blossoms sway
From leafless boughs across that dreamy grey.

O world, how worthy of a golden age !
How might Theocritus have sung and found
The Oreads here, the Naiads gathering round,
Their pallid locks still dripping to the ground !

For me, O world, thou art how mere a stage,
Whereon the human soul must act alone,
In a dead language, with the plot unknown,
Nor learn what happens when the play is done.

Old Songs.

THIS song I wrote—ah me, how long ago !
    When up the stair of Heaven and down again
    (For even then I did not long remain),
With happy feet I used to come and go.

This ode I sang beneath a laurel-bough
    Where I had sought for Truth among the dead ;
    This little verse (and still the page is red),
To soothe some easier pang forgotten now.

I took the dew of lilies grown apart ;
    The scanty wine of Amphoras; and, bright
And clear, the blood that flows from trivial scars ;

But with the bitter ink of mine own heart
    I have not written and I must not write,
        Let rust and acid dim the eternal stars.

Versailles.

" *Le monde est l'œuvre d'un grand Architecte qui est mort avant de l'avoir achevé.*"

B. CONSTANT.

THE king is dead who planned these terraces ;
    The turf has grown to meadow-grass again ;
The lake is rank beneath the untended trees,
    And down the mouldering statues drips the rain.

The king is dead. Ay, he, with all his kind,
    Is absolutely vanished, lost, and gone,
And not a trace of him remains behind ;
    But the forsaken palace lingers on.

How desolate ! The weary waters drowned
    In mist, the empty alleys chill and frore,
The vast and melancholy pleasure-ground
    Where the forgotten monarch comes no more.

How like an older Folly, planned no less
    For beauty, where a greater monarch trod,
And now, grown old, in its extreme distress
    Abandoned by the long-departed God !

Oct., 1888.

F *

Melancholia.

(For an engraving by Albrecht Dürer.)

SO many years I toiled like Caliban
  To fetch the stones and earth to build my
    fane ;
So many years I thought before the brain
Reluctant would divulge the final plan.

Years upon years to forge the invented tools
  Novel, as all my temple should be new ;
  Years upon years to fashion and to hew
The stones that should astound a world of fools.

Now shall I build ? *Cui bono ?*—lo, the salt
  Hath lost its savour and I have no will :
What reck I now of gate or dome or vault ?

Among the ruins of the thing undone
  I sit and ask myself *Cui bono ?* till
The sun sets, and a bat flies past the sun.

Under the Trees.

I LAY full length near lonely trees
Heart-full of sighing silences;
So far as eyes could see all round
There was no life, no stir, no sound.

I thought no more down in the grass
Of all that must be or that was;
My weary brain forgot to ache,
My heart was still and did not break.

So close I lay to earth's large breast
I could have dreamed myself at rest;
Only that then the grass must be
Above instead of under me

Wherefore, I thought, should I regain
My anxious life that is so vain?
Here will I lie, forgetting strife,
Till death shall end this death-in-life.

Ah, no : because, O coward will,
Thy destined work thou must fulfil,
Because no soul, be it great or small,
Can rise alone or lonely fall.

Therefore the old war must not cease,
The hard old inner war of peace,
With heart and body and mind and soul
Each striving for a different goal.

Therefore I will arise and bear
The burden all men everywhere
Have borne and must bear, and bear yet,
Till the end come when we forget.

Fire-flies.

I.

TO-NIGHT I watch the fire-flies rise
    And shine along the air ;
They float beneath the starry skies,
    As mystical and fair,
Over the hedge where dimly glows
The deep gold of the Persian rose.

I watch the fire-flies drift and float :
    Each is a dreamy flame,
Star-coloured each, a starry mote,
    Like stars not all the same ;
But whiter some, or faintly green,
Or wannest blue was ever seen.

They cross and cross and disappear,
    And then again they glow ;
Still drifting faintly there and here,
    Still crossing to and fro,
As though in all their wandering
They wove a wide and shining thing.

II.

O fire-flies, would I knew the weft
  You have the weaving of!
For, as I watch you move, bereft
  Of thought or will or love,
I fear, O listless flames, you weave
The fates of men who strive and grieve.

The web of life, the weft of dreams,
  You weave it ceaselessly;
A strange and filmy thing it seems,
  And made in mystery
Of wind and darkness threaded through
With light these heavens never knew.

O pale, mysterious, wandering fire,
  Born of the earth, alive
With the same breath that I respire,
  Who know and think and strive;
You circle round me, stranger far
Than any charm of any star!

III.

Ah me, as faint as you, as slight,
  As hopelessly remote
As you, who still across the night

Innumerably float,
Intangible as you, I see
The motives of our destiny.

For ah, no angel of the stars,
   No guardian of the soul,
Stoops down beyond the heavenly bars
   Our courses to control.
But filled and nourished with our breath
Are the dim hands that weave our death.

They weave with many threads our souls,
   A subtle-tinted thing,
So interwoven that none controls
   His own imagining ;
For every strand with other strands
They twine and bind with viewless hands.

They weave the future of the past ;
   Their mystic web is wrought
With dreams from which we woke at last,
   And many a secret thought ;
For still they weave, howe'er we strive,
The web new-woven for none alive.

IV.

And still the fire-flies come and go—
  Each is a dreamy flame—
Still palely drifting to and fro
  The very way they came—
As though, across the dark they wove
Fate and the shining web thereof.

Yet, even were I sure of it,
  I would not lift a hand
To break the threads that shine and flit—
  For, ah, I understand :
Ruin, indeed, I well might leave ;
But a new web could never weave.

Spring.

SPRING, the tender maiden,
  Like a girl who greets her lover,
Comes, her apron laden
  Deep with flower and leaf we liked of old ;
Not a sprig forgetting
  That we then demanded of her ;
Changing not nor setting
  Out of place the tiniest frill or fold.

See, the aspen still is
  Hung awry to droop and falter ;
Still the leaves of lilies
  Lift aloft their tall and tender sheath.
Wiser than the sages,
  Spring would never dare to alter
What so many ages
  Showed already right in bloom and wreath.

Ah, could Spring remember
   Every thrill and fancy perished
In the soul's December ;
   Lost for ever, faded from the truth !
Holy things and tender,
   Dead, alas ! however cherished.
Breathe, O Spring, and render
   That forgotten radiance of our youth !

Sacrifice.

O PATIENT-EYED and tender saint,
   Too far from thee I stand,
With vain desires perplexed and faint ;
   Reach out thy helping hand.
No fire is on the holy hill,
   No voice on Sinai now ;
But, in our gloom and darkness still
   Abiding, help me thou.

They move on whom thy light is shed
   Through lives of larger scope ;
For them beneath the false and dead
   There stirs a quickening hope.
So on some gusty morn we mark
   The reddening tops of trees,
And hear in carols of the lark
   Thespesian promises.

Writing History.

THE profit of my living long ago
　　I dedicated to the unloving dead,
Though all my service they shall never know
　　Whose world is vanished and their name unsaid.

For none remembers now the good, the ill
　　They did, the deeds they thought should last
　　　　for aye :
But in the little room my voice can fill
　　They shall not be forgotten till I die.

So, in a lonely churchyard by the shore,
　　The sea winds drift the sand across the mounds
And those forgotten graves are found no more,
　　And no man knows the churchyard's holy
　　　　bounds ;

Till one come by and stoop with reverent hands
To clear the graves of their encumbering sands.

The Alembic.

IN this alembic have I cast my youth,
  For here I do believe if anywhere,
  Here where the fires of death burn all things
    bare
I may distil the eternal gold of Truth.

Therefore the future is an empty name,
  And life to me a dream that will not last,
  And all my care is only for the Past,
Veiled with the veil of no man's ruth or shame.

Yea, Death, that hast the secret Life withholds,
  Thy meek and patient servitor am I ;
    And from thine alchemy I will not cease
    Until I find amid thine essences,
Writ in a little sand of divers golds,
  The answer to the eternal How and Why.

The Wall.

THE sun falls through the olive-trees
 And shines upon the wall below,
 And lights the wall which cannot know
The Sunlight that it never sees.

I lie and dream ; the Eternal Mind
 Rains down on me and fills me full
 With secrets high and wonderful ;
And still my soul is deaf and blind.

The Idea.

BENEATH this world of stars and flowers
    That rolls in visible deity,
I dream another world is ours
    And is the soul of all we see.

It hath no form, it hath no spirit;
    It is perchance the Eternal Mind;
Beyond the sense that we inherit
    I feel it dim and undefined.

How far below the depth of being,
    How wide beyond the starry bound
It rolls unconscious and unseeing,
    And is as Number or as Sound.

And through the vast fantastic visions
    Of all this actual universe,
It moves unswerved by our decisions,
    And is the play that we rehearse.

The Ideal.

THE night is dark and warm and very still,
  Only the moon goes pallid and alone ;
The moon and I the whole wide heavens fill,
  And all the earth lies little, lost, unknown.

I walk along the byways of my Soul,
  Beyond the streets where all the world may go,
Until at last I reach the hidden goal
  Built up in strength where only I may know.

For in my Soul a temple have I made,
  Set on a height, divine and steep and far,
Nor often may I hope those floors to tread,
  Or reach the gates that glimmer like a star.

O secret, inner shining of my dream,
  How clear Thou risest on my soul to-night !
Forth will I fare and seek the heavenly beam,
  And stand within the precincts of the light.

And I will press beyond the curtain'd door,
  And up the empty aisle where no one sings ;
There will I fall before thee and adore,
  And feel the shadowy winnowing of thy wings.

So will I reach thee, Spirit; for I have known
  Thy voice, and looked upon thy blinding eyes ;
And well thou knowest the world to me is grown
  One dimness whence thy dreamy beacons rise.

Nor ask I any hope nor any end,
  That thus for thee I dream all day, all night ;
But, like the moon along the skies, I wend,
  Knowing no world below my borrowed light.

God in a Heart.

I.

ONCE, where the unentered Temple stood, at
  noon
No sun-ray pierced the dim unwindowed aisle;
And all the flooding whiteness of the moon
  Could only bathe the outer peristyle.

And as we passed we praised the Temple front;
  But one went in; with careless feet he trod
The long-forgotten pavement moss'd and blunt
  And found the altar of the unprayed-to God.

He reached and lit the tapers of the shrine
  And let their radiance flood the vault obscure;
But ah! upon what evil things to shine,
  Blind, crawling, chill, discoloured, and impure.

And as the Light burns clearer through the gloom,
  More foul, more deathly, shows the illumined
    room.

II.

O light of God, lit in the heart of man,
  More welcome than the well in desert sands,
We bless thee fallen hither for a span
  To glorify the Temple made with hands.

We did not deem how foul the Temple was,
  Until thou visitedst the untended shrine ;
Thy glory is not peace for us, alas,
  Illumination tragic and divine.

Yet unrelenting pour, revealing Light !
  Scare and annihilate all our blind desires,
Shine through our thoughts, and purify the night,
  And burn us clean with thy transcendent fires,

Until thou leavest us renewed and whole
Thy mortal Temple of the transient Soul.

Calais Beacon.

(*To E. S.*)

FOR long before we came upon the coast and
the line of the surge,
Pale on the uttermost verge,
We saw the great white rays that lay along the air
on high
Between us and the sky.

So soft they lay, so pure and still : " Those are the
ways," you said,
" Only the angels tread ; "
And long we watched them tremble past the hurry-
ing rush of the train
Over the starlit plain.

Until at last we saw the strange, pallid, electrical
star
Burning wanly afar :
The lighthouse beacon sending out its rays on
either hand,
Over the sea and the land.

Those pale and filmy rays that reach to mariners,
    lost in the night,
    A hope of dawn and a light—
How soft and vague they lie along the darkness
    shrouding o'er
    The dim sea and the shore.

And many fall in vain across the untenanted
    marshes to die,
    And few where sailors cry ;
Yet, though the moon go out in clouds, and all of
    the stars grow wan,
    Their pale light shineth on.

O souls, that save a world by night, ye too are no
    rays of the noon,
    And no inconstant moon ;
But such pale, tender-shining things as yon faint
    beacon afar,
    Whiter than any star.

No planet names that all may tell, no meteor
    radiance and glow,
    For a wondering world to know.
You shine as pale and soft as that, you pierce the
    stormy night,
    And know not of your light !

The Mushrooms of the Mine.

DEEP in the mines of the North, in the centre
  of desolate Sweden,
  More than a mile underground, winter has never
  an end—
Lo, not a rift in the granite mass of the mountain
  where ever
  Ray or dew of the morn, dream of the moon,
  may descend.

Up in the hills overhead the spring and the summer are mingled ;
  Lilacs heavy with blossom o'ershadow the
  ripening corn.
How should the hollow heart of the mountain
  thrill with the shiver
  Rippling swift in the leaves when the first of the
  roses is born ?

Six months long, overhead, the bright white sun of
the Vikings
Glitters clear and immense, seven-rayed as a
star.
Cold and clear as a star of steel—see, it pierces the
midnight;
Crystal, undazzling, eterne. . . . Ay, but the
mine is too far!

Yet in the depth of the mine where the day and
the night never enter,
Lo! in the mine there is light, and lo! there are
flowers in the mine!
Woven of dew and of moonlight, blooming in pale
phosphorescence,
Moon-blue, rose as the levin, green as the
marish-shine.

Hanging aloft from the roof of the wonderful
flower-lighted caverns,
Shedding hither and thither their flakes of the
milkiest flame.
Light that is not of the earth and not of the
heavens exhaling:
These are the stars of the miners; out of the
darkness they came.

Mushrooms of the mine—no more—that the sun
    never visits,
Born of the ooze and the damp, bred in the slime
    and the cold,
Scentless and petalless blossoms, made without
    pleasure and hidden :
  See, how they shed in the darkness the light
    they shall never behold !

1890.

An Orchard at Avignon.

THE hills are white, but not with snow :
   They are as pale in summer time,
For herb or grass may never grow
   Upon their slopes of lime.

Within the circle of the hills
   A ring, all flowering in a round,
An orchard-ring of almond fills
   The plot of stony ground.

More fair than happier trees, I think,
   Grown in well-watered pasture land,
These parched and stunted branches, pink
   Above the stones and sand.

O white, austere, ideal place,
   Where very few will care to come,
Where spring hath lost the waving grace
   She wears for us at home !

Fain would I sit and watch for hours
  The holy whiteness of thy hills,
Their wreath of pale auroral flowers,
  Their peace the silence fills.

A place of secret peace thou art,
  Such peace as in an hour of pain
One moment fills the amazed heart,
  And never comes again.

Twilight.

WHEN I was young the twilight seemed too
long.

How often on the western window seat
  I leaned my book against the misty pane
  And spelled the last enchanting lines again,
The while my mother hummed an ancient song,
Or sighed a little and said: " The hour is sweet ! "
When I, rebellious, clamoured for the light.

But now I love the soft approach of night,
  And now with folded hands I sit and dream
  While all too fleet the hours of twilight seem ;
And thus I know that I am growing old.

O granaries of Age ! O manifold
And royal harvest of the common years !
There are in all thy treasure-house no ways
But lead by soft descent and gradual slope
To memories more exquisite than Hope.
Thine is the Iris born of olden tears,

And thrice more happy are the happy days
That live divinely in thy lingering rays.
So autumn roses bear a lovelier flower ;
So in the emerald after-sunset hour
The orchard wall and trembling aspen trees
Appear an infinite Hesperides.
Ay, as at dusk we sit with folded hands,
Who knows, who cares in what enchanted lands
We wander while the undying memories throng ?

When I was young the twilight seemed too long.

1889.

Darwinism.

WHEN first the unflowering Fern forest
  Shadowed the dim lagoons of old,
A vague, unconscious, long unrest
  Swayed the great fronds of green and gold.

Until the flexible stem grew rude,
  The fronds began to branch and bower,
And lo ! upon the unblossoming wood
  There breaks a dawn of apple-flower.

Then on the fruitful forest-boughs
  For ages long the unquiet ape
Swung happy in his airy house
  And plucked the apple, and sucked the grape.

Until at length in him there stirred
  The old, unchanged, remote distress,
That pierced his world of wind and bird
  With some divine unhappiness.

Not love, nor the wild fruits he sought,
   Nor the fierce battles of his clan
Could still the unborn and aching thought
   Until the brute became the man.

Long since. . . . And now the same unrest
   Goads to the same invisible goal,
Till some new gift, undreamed, unguessed
   End the new travail of the soul.

Antiphon to the Holy Spirit.

Men and Women sing.

Men.

O THOU that movest all, O Power
　　That bringest life where'er Thou art,
O Breath of God in star and flower,
　　Mysterious aim of soul and heart ;
Within the thought that cannot grasp Thee
　　In its unfathomable hold,
We worship Thee who may not clasp Thee,
　　O God, unreckoned and untold !

Women.

O Source and Sea of Love, O Spirit
　　That makest every soul akin,
O Comforter whom we inherit,
　　We turn and worship Thee within !
To give beyond all dreams of giving,
　　To lose ourselves as Thou in us,
We long ; for Thou, O Fount of living,
　　Art lost in Thy creation thus !

Men.

The mass of unborn matter knew Thee,
  And lo ! the splendid, silent sun
Sprang out to be a witness to Thee
  Who art the All, who art the One ;
The airy plants unseen that flourish
  Their floating strands of filmy rose,
Too small for sight, are Thine to nourish ;
  For Thou art all that breathes and grows.

Women.

Thou art the ripening of the fallows,
  The swelling of the buds in rain ;
Thou art the joy of birth that hallows
  The rending of the flesh in twain ;
O Life, O Love, how undivided
  Thou broodest o'er this world of Thine,
Obscure and strange, yet surely guided
  To reach a distant end divine !

Men.

We know Thee in the doubt and terror
  That reels before the world we see ;
We knew Thee in the faiths of error ;
  We know Thee most who most are free.

This phantom of the world around Thee
Is vast, divine, but not the whole :
We worship Thee, and we have found Thee
In all that satisfies the soul !

Men and Women.

How shall we serve, how shall we own Thee,
O breath of Love and Life and Thought ?
How shall we praise, who are not shown Thee ?
How shall we serve, who are as nought ?
Ah, though Thy worlds maintain unbroken
The silence of their awful round,
A voice within our souls hath spoken,
And we who seek have more than found.

Epilogue.

IN the cup of life, 'tis true,
　　Dwells a draught of bitter dew—

Disenchantment, sorrow, pain,
　　Hunger that no bread can still,
Dreary dawns that dawn in vain,
　　Hopes that torture, joys that kill.

Yet no other cup I know
Where such radiant waters glow :

It contains the song of birds,
　　And the shining of the sun ;
And the sweet unspoken words
　　We have dreamed of, every one ;

Love of women, minds of men.—
—Take the cup, nor break it, then.

The Gresham Press,

UNWIN BROTHERS,

CHILWORTH AND LONDON.

✝